WRESTLING SUPERST★RS

TRIPLE H

BY JESSE ARMSTRONG

EPIC

BELLWETHER MEDIA • MINNEAPOLIS, MN

EPIC BOOKS are no ordinary books. They burst with intense action, high-speed heroics, and shadows of the unknown. Are you ready for an Epic adventure?

This edition first published in 2015 by Bellwether Media, Inc.

No part of this publication may be reproduced in whole or in part without written permission of the publisher. For information regarding permission, write to Bellwether Media, Inc., Attention: Permissions Department, 5357 Penn Avenue South, Minneapolis, MN 55419.

Library of Congress Cataloging-in-Publication Data

Armstrong, Jesse.
  Triple H / by Jesse Armstrong.
      pages cm. – (Epic. Wrestling Superstars)
  Includes bibliographical references and index.
  Summary: "Engaging images accompany information about Triple H. The combination of high-interest subject matter and light text is intended for students in grades 2 through 7"– Provided by publisher.
  Audience: Age: 7-12.
  ISBN 978-1-62617-183-1 (hardcover : alk. paper)
  1. Triple H., 1969–Juvenile literature. 2. Wrestlers–United States–Biography–Juvenile literature. I. Title.
  GV1196.T75A76 2015
  796.812092–dc23
  [B]
                        2014041514

Printed in the United States of America, North Mankato, MN.

TABLE OF CONTENTS

THE DEBUT 4

WHO IS TRIPLE H? 8

LIFE BEFORE WWE 10

A WWE SUPERSTAR 14

WINNING MOVES 18

GLOSSARY 22

TO LEARN MORE 23

INDEX 24

WARNING!

The wrestling moves used in this book are performed by professionals.
Do not attempt to reenact any of the moves performed in this book.

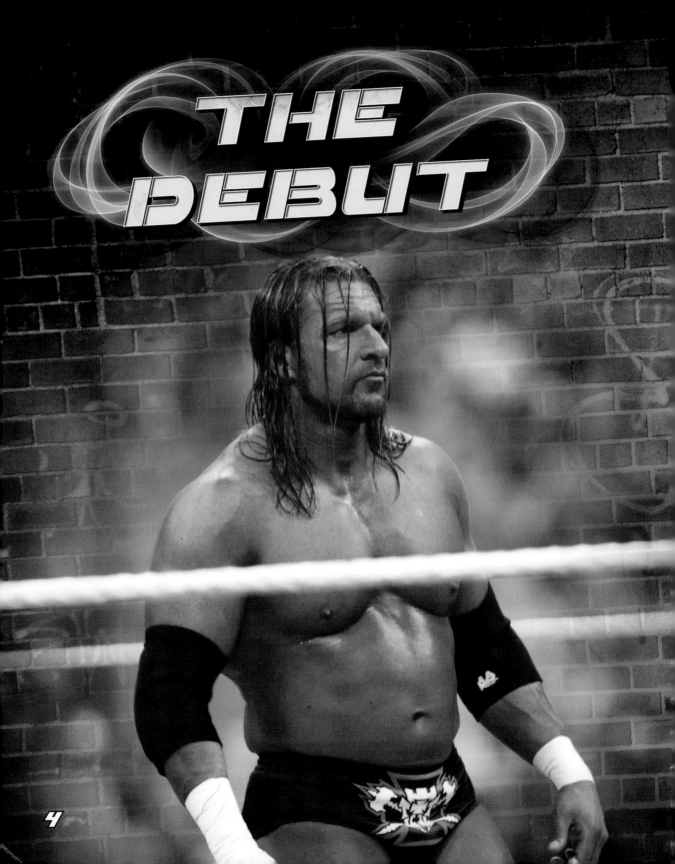

THE DEBUT

Triple H walks to the ring like a **noble**.
He is dressed in classy clothes. He has a
proud **posture** for his **debut**.

Triple H takes off his white button-down shirt. Then he tries to take down Buck Zumhoff. But Zumhoff puts up a fight. Eventually Triple H pins Zumhoff with a **leg hook**.

HHH
★

Triple H stands for
Hunter Hearst Helmsley.

WHO IS TRIPLE H?

Triple H is WWE's King of Kings. He has **reigned** as a champion many times during the past two **decades**. His power reaches outside of the ring, too. He has held WWE **executive** positions.

BIG BUSINESSMAN
★

His job titles have included
Chief Operating Officer and
Executive Vice President
of Talent.

LIFE BEFORE WWE

MAJOR MUSCLES

At age 19, Triple H won the Teen Mr. New Hampshire bodybuilding contest.

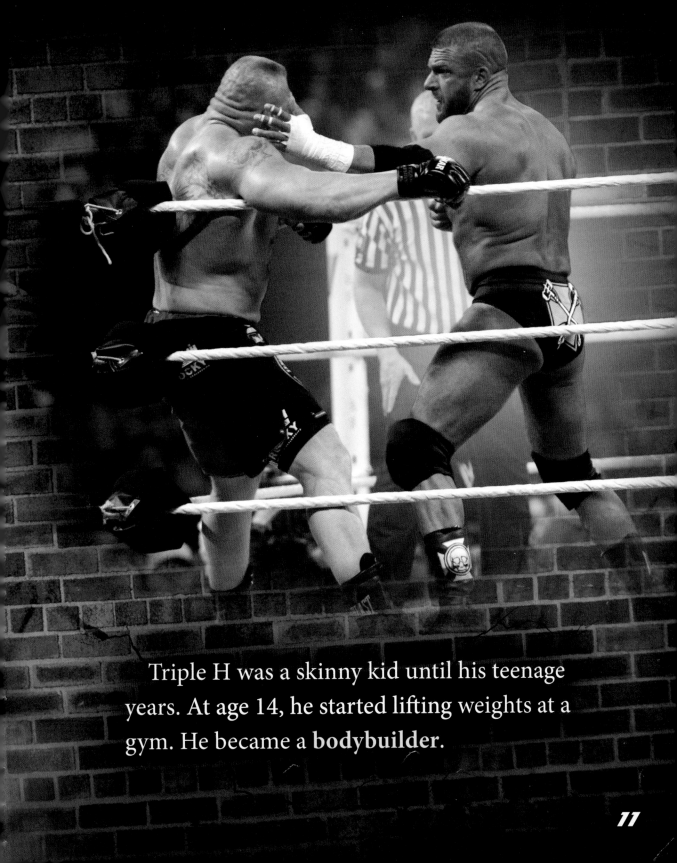

Triple H was a skinny kid until his teenage years. At age 14, he started lifting weights at a gym. He became a **bodybuilder**.

Then Triple H went to pro wrestling school in Massachusetts. In 1994, he joined World Championship Wrestling (WCW). He wrestled as Terra Ryzing and Frenchman Jean-Paul Levesque.

A WWE SUPERSTAR

STAR PROFILE

WRESTLING NAME: Triple H

REAL NAME: Paul Michael Levesque

BIRTHDATE: July 27, 1969

HOMETOWN: Nashua, New Hampshire

HEIGHT: 6 feet, 4 inches (1.9 meters)

WEIGHT: 255 pounds (116 kilograms)

WWE DEBUT: 1995

FINISHING MOVE: Pedigree

Triple H entered WWE in 1995 as Hunter
Hearst Helmsley. Fans treated him like a **heel**.
Eventually he nicknamed himself The Game.
This declared his importance.

In 2001, Triple H suffered a bad muscle tear.
After he healed, fans welcomed him back.
He then continued his winning ways.

WINNING MOVES

SPINEBUSTER

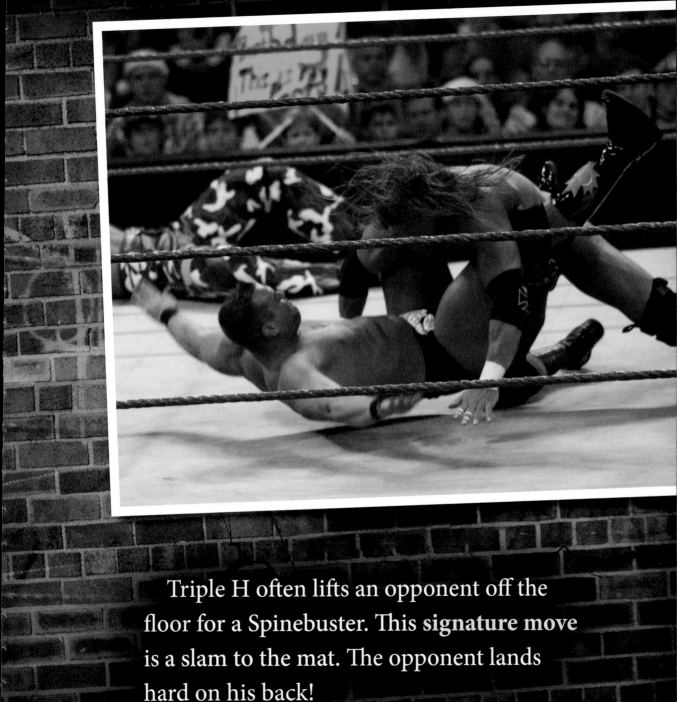

Triple H often lifts an opponent off the
floor for a Spinebuster. This **signature** move
is a slam to the mat. The opponent lands
hard on his back!

PEDIGREE

The **Pedigree** is Triple H's **finishing move**. He shoves a wrestler's head between his legs. Then he locks the wrestler's arms. He jumps up and lands on his knees. Face-plant!

GLOSSARY

bodybuilder—a person who lifts weights and eats in a way to build muscle

debut—first official appearance

decades—periods of ten years

executive—relating to the leadership of a company or organization

finishing move—a wrestling move that finishes off an opponent

heel—a wrestler viewed as a villain

leg hook—a pin in which one wrestler locks his arm around another wrestler's leg

noble—a person of high social standing

pedigree—the record of upper-class roots

posture—the look of the body while standing or sitting

reigned—held an important title for a period of time

signature move—a move that a wrestler is famous for performing

TO LEARN MORE

At the Library

Armstrong, Jesse. *Randy Orton*. Minneapolis, Minn.:
Bellwether Media, 2015.

Black, Jake. *WWE General Manager's Handbook*. New York,
N.Y.: Grosset & Dunlap, 2012.

West, Tracey. *Race to the Rumble*. New York, N.Y.: Grosset &
Dunlap, 2011.

On the Web

Learning more about Triple H
is as easy as 1, 2, 3.

1. Go to www.factsurfer.com.

2. Enter "Triple H" into the search box.

3. Click the "Surf" button and you will see a list
of related web sites.

With factsurfer.com, finding more information
is just a click away.

INDEX

bodybuilding, 10, 11

debut, 5

executive positions, 8, 9

finishing move, 21

heel, 15

leg hook, 6

Massachusetts, 12

mat, 19

names, 7, 12, 15

nicknames, 8, 15

noble, 5

Pedigree, 20, 21

ring, 5, 8

school, 12

signature move, 19

Spinebuster, 18, 19

Teen Mr. New Hampshire, 10

World Championship
    Wrestling (WCW), 12

WWE, 8, 15

Zumhoff, Buck, 6